BE STRONG

Pat Zietlow Miller
Illustrated by Jen Hill

Roaring Brook Press
New York

To the first two teachers who told me I was a strong writer:
Chloe Wandschneider and Jill Mueller
—P. Z. M.

For Rosie

—J. H.

Published by Roaring Brook Press
Roaring Brook Press is a division of Holtzbrinck Publishing Holdings Limited Partnership
120 Broadway, New York, NY 10271 • mackids.com

Library of Congress Cataloging-in-Publication Data
Names: Miller, Pat Zietlow, author. | Hill, Jen, 1975- illustrator.
Title: Be strong / Pat Zietlow Miller ; illustrated by Jen Hill.
Description: First edition. | New York : Roaring Brook Press, 2021. |
Audience: Ages 3-6. | Audience: Grades K-1. |
Summary: Not strong enough to ascend the climbing wall at school, a discouraged child
learns that there are other ways to be strong, from not giving up when working for a good
cause or learning a new skill to making sure that no one sits alone in the lunchroom.
Identifiers: LCCN 2020039916 | ISBN 9781250221117 (hardcover)
Subjects: CYAC: Conduct of life—Fiction.
Classification: LCC PZ7.M63224 Bh 2021 | DDC [E]—dc23
LC record available at https://lccn.loc.gov/2020039916

Our books may be purchased in bulk for promotional, educational, or business use.
Please contact your local bookseller or the Macmillan Corporate and Premium Sales Department
at (800) 221-7945 ext. 5442 or by email at MacmillanSpecialMarkets@macmillan.com.

First edition, 2021 • Book design by Jen Keenan
The illustrations in this book were created with gouache on paper and retouched with Adobe Photoshop.
Printed in China by RR Donnelley Asia Printing Solutions Ltd., Dongguan City, Guangdong Province

1 3 5 7 9 10 8 6 4 2

My school gym has tall walls.
I never noticed them before.
But today, I have to climb them.

Cayla scrambles to the top like it's no big deal.

When she gets there, she laughs and flexes her muscles.

I don't reach the top.
Or laugh.

My muscles keep me stuck
at the bottom.

I'm not strong.

Some days, I can't even lift my backpack.

Other days, simple things seem too hard.

My family says being strong gets you through life.

When hard times happen and things don't go as planned.

So I ask, "How can I be strong?"

Dad says being strong means showing up.

Like when our neighborhood wakes up early
to help people who have lost their homes.

We're tired, but everyone packs and carries.
We collect clothing, cots, and cans of food.
When I see how we can help, I don't miss sleeping in.

Mama says being strong means speaking up.
Like when she sees a corner that needs
a crossing guard.

She asks city leaders.

They say: "No."

But Mama knows she's right.
She talks to friends and neighbors—
even the mayor—then asks again.

Grandma Zee says being strong means not giving up.

Like when she started running.

At first, she barely jogged a block.
She worried people would laugh.
But she keeps going.

Day after day.
Block after block.
Even when it rains.

I want to be strong.

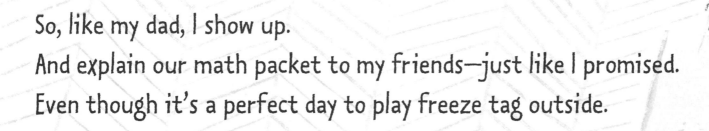

So, like my dad, I show up.

And explain our math packet to my friends—just like I promised.

Even though it's a perfect day to play freeze tag outside.

Like Mama, I speak up.
When I see kids looking lonely at lunch, I want to help.

I think of an idea and tell my teacher.
The principal, too!

Then we make a special table
so no one sits alone.

Some kids say it's weird.
But that doesn't stop us.

make
a
friend
:)

And like Grandma Zee, I do not give up.

The first time I play my accordion,
it makes screeching sounds.
My ears hurt. My eyes water.
I don't think I'll ever get it.
But I sign up for the talent show anyway.

And each time I practice,

it sounds a little more like music.

Dad says . . .

Being strong means knowing you can make things happen.
And turn nothing into something.

Like when I want to dress up as some of my heroes.
I decide to reduce, reuse, and recycle.

So I look around
and use my imagination.

It's harder than buying a costume.
And it's not perfect.

But I make this happen.

Mama says . . .

Being strong means moving forward.

"Tiny steps are fine," she says. "As long as they take you in the right direction."

When I decide to write one hundred thank-you notes to strong people, it seems like so many!
More than I could ever do.

But whenever I give one away, I'm closer to my goal.

Grandma Zee says . . .

Strong people care. And sometimes cry.
They help people, and let other people help them.

That's why,
when Cayla offers me a hand,

I take it.

I don't reach the top,
but I get higher than before.

So I say . . .

I am strong.

And when I'm not strong enough alone,
I can be strong with someone else.

Like Grandma Zee and me.
When we each take a backpack strap,

flex our muscles,

and lift.

Together, we'll keep going strong.

Until everyone is showing up.
Speaking up.

And never, ever
giving up.